Kindness is Cool!

Bobbie Kalman

Crabtree Publishing Company
www.crabtreebooks.com

Be Your Best SELF
Building Social-Emotional Skills

Created by Bobbie Kalman

For my cousin, Heather Christine Brissenden,
who is the kindest person I know, as well as the best singer.
I love your ideas and music—especially River of Dreams!

Author and Editor-in-Chief
Bobbie Kalman

Editor
Kathy Middleton

Proofreader
Crystal Sikkens

Photo research
Bobbie Kalman

Design
Bobbie Kalman
Katherine Berti
Samantha Crabtree
(text and cover)

Print and production coordinator
Katherine Berti

Images:
© iStockphoto.com: front cover; page 18 (top); page 24 (top letters); page 25 (top right); page 27 (bottom right)
© Shutterstock.com: all other photographs and images

Library and Archives Canada Cataloguing in Publication

Title: Kindness is cool! / Bobbie Kalman.
Names: Kalman, Bobbie, author.
Description: Series statement: Be your best self: building social-emotional skills | Includes index.
Identifiers: Canadiana (print) 20190134453 | Canadiana (ebook) 20190134461 | ISBN 9780778767084 (hardcover) | ISBN 9780778767183 (softcover) | ISBN 9781427124197 (HTML)
Subjects: LCSH: Kindness—Juvenile literature. | LCSH: Compassion—Juvenile literature. | LCSH: Generosity—Juvenile literature. | LCSH: Conduct of life—Juvenile literature.
Classification: LCC BJ1533.K5 K35 2019 | DDC j177/.7—dc23

Library of Congress Cataloging-in-Publication Data

Names: Kalman, Bobbie, author.
Title: Kindness is cool! / Bobbie Kalman.
Description: New York : Crabtree Publishing Company, 2020. | Series: Be your best self: building social-emotional skills | Includes index.
Identifiers: LCCN 2019023858 (print) | LCCN 2019023859 (ebook) | ISBN 9780778767084 (hardcover) | ISBN 9780778767183 (paperback) | ISBN 9781427124197 (ebook)
Subjects: LCSH: Kindness--Juvenile literature. | Conduct of life--Juvenile literature.
Classification: LCC BJ1533.K5 K35 2020 (print) | LCC BJ1533.K5 (ebook) | DDC 177/.7--dc23
LC record available at https://lccn.loc.gov/2019023858
LC ebook record available at https://lccn.loc.gov/2019023859

Crabtree Publishing Company
www.crabtreebooks.com 1-800-387-7650

Printed in the U.S.A./102019/CG20190809

Published in Canada
Crabtree Publishing
616 Welland Ave.
St. Catharines, Ontario
L2M 5V6

Published in the United States
Crabtree Publishing
PMB 59051
350 Fifth Avenue, 59th Floor
New York, New York 10118

Published in the United Kingdom
Crabtree Publishing
Maritime House
Basin Road North, Hove
BN41 1WR

Published in Australia
Crabtree Publishing
Unit 3 – 5 Currumbin Court
Capalaba
QLD 4157

Contents

What is kindness?

Kindness is treating other people in a gentle and caring way, the way you like to be treated. It is doing things for others without being asked or expecting anything in return. When you are kind to someone, not only does the other person feel good, but you also feel good about yourself. You want to be around people who are kind to you. Being kind at home, school, and in your **community** makes those places peaceful and happy for you and others.

Kindness words

You can show kindness by smiling, giving compliments, sharing, being grateful, and helping others. With a group of friends, discuss what the words below mean and how they can help you be happy and kind to yourself and others.

The Butterfly Effect

The butterfly effect is an idea that **illustrates**, or shows, how a small change in the present can make a huge change in the future. For example, the simple flap of a butterfly's wings now might lead to an enormous windstorm later. Small acts of kindness can lead to big changes in our lives and the lives of others. Something you say or do today could have a huge **impact**, or effect, on your future or the future of others. Many years ago, a kind teacher told one of her students, who was from another country and just learning English, that she was a good writer. That inspired the student to go on to become the author of hundreds of books!

Think of yourself as a butterfly that can spread kindness to others near and far. You will make the world a much happier place for those who need love and kindness in their lives. Write down all the kind things you have done and imagine each one as a butterfly. Then write down any results you think may have started with your acts of kindness.

Think of some kind thoughts you could "flap" to people who need it. As you read this book, think of ways that you can best spread your kindness in your school and community.

A kind and happy you

Happiness is **contagious**! If you are happy, you will want to make others happy, too. As kindness butterflies, we can make a big difference to those around us, and even those who are far away. When we believe in ourselves, we feel good about others. Knowing what makes you feel sad means you can do something to change it. Becoming **aware** of other people's feelings is also very important. You can help others be happy or ease their pain if you know how they feel. We all want to be happy, but we are different in how happy we choose to be.

My friends and I love to play soccer! It makes us feel happy.

Are you happy?

Some people are able to be happy most of the time, no matter what problems they have. Other people find it hard to be happy. A person who has everything he or she needs might not be as happy as a person who has very little. We shouldn't rely on other people or things to make us happy. True happiness can only come from inside. We can find happiness by doing the things we love. What activities or hobbies do you enjoy? Try practicing them every day. You could also join groups that enjoy doing the same things you like to do, such as music or sports. The children below have fun spending time together at a playground.

Learning about emotions

Our emotions have the power to make us feel both good and bad. Sometimes we get so concerned about how others see us, that we forget who we really are. We are afraid of being different and feel that others will not accept us. We might think that we are not good enough. These things can make it hard to love ourselves, but love does not start with others—it starts with us. Learning to recognize why you feel a certain way will help you figure out how to manage your emotions in a positive way. It will also help you understand why others feel the way they do. It all starts with the important task of learning to love yourself!

How do you feel?

Do you sometimes feel angry, afraid, sad, worried, lonely, upset, or disappointed?

- What story are you telling yourself about why you feel this way?
- How are you showing your feelings?
- What do you think you need right now to change this feeling?
- How can you change your thoughts from negative to positive? You can start by taking deep breaths, thinking happy thoughts, or going for a walk.

Your happiness test

To find out how true-to-yourself you are, ask yourself these questions:

- Do you often feel sorry for yourself?
- Do you say "no" more often than you say "yes"?
- Are you thankful for your health, family, home, friends, and the things you own?
- What activities make you feel happy? How often do you do them?

It's OK! I'm OK!

- I'm OK. I'm perfect the way I am.
- It's OK to be different.
- It's OK to ignore bullies and walk away from them.
- It's OK to make mistakes.
- It's OK to have problems. I am good at solving problems.
- It's OK to ask friends, parents, or teachers for help when I need it.

How many acts of kindness do you do each day? Start a kindness journal and write down each act of kindness that you did that day. Also write down acts of kindness done by others. How might these acts of kindness cause a butterfly effect?

Kindness to our bodies

When we are healthy, we feel happy, too. What do you need to have a healthy body and mind? You need sunshine, clean air to breathe, clean water to drink, and at least ten hours of sleep. Being healthy also means eating foods that are good for you.

*Healthy foods include vegetables, fruits, and whole grains. Foods that are not good for us contain a lot of sugar, salt, and **ingredients** that are hard to read or pronounce.*

Going for a walk with your family or friends is a great way to get fresh air, as well as exercise. Exercise is important to both our bodies and minds.

More than half of your body is made up of water. You need to drink at least six glasses of water each day. You also need to get plenty of sleep!

We need to be fit!

To be healthy, you need to be fit. Being fit means having a strong, healthy body that is able to do the things you want and need it to do. To be fit, you must exercise the muscles in your body. Your heart is a muscle, too. Exercise that gets your heart pumping helps keep your heart healthy. Which are your favorite exercises? Which make you feel calm and happy?

Know what safety equipment you need and always wear or use it.

How active are you?

Getting fit starts with being more active. To make exercising more fun, find a group of friends who also want to be more active and discuss ways that you can become fit together. Here are some ways you can get started.

- Choose a physical activity you think is fun and do it often.
- As your body gets more fit, try activities that move your body in different ways.
- Be active at least one hour each day. Walking and running are great **cardio exercises** that make your heart stronger.
- **Strength exercises** build your muscles so they don't get tired as quickly. Swimming, doing pushups and situps, and lifting small weights are great ways to build muscles.
- **Flexibility exercises** stretch your muscles in different ways so they don't feel sore.

Gymnastics exercises are good for flexibility. They also build muscles. Gymnastics and dancing are great for your heart, as well.

Kindness to my family

Families can be very different. They often include parents, grandparents, and children, but not all families are made up of the same combination of people. Some **extended** families live together. Extended families can include grandparents, aunts and uncles, and stepchildren. Some families may have only one parent, and others may have children who were **adopted** into the family after they were born. No matter what kind of family you are part of, each family is a community. People who are part of a family community live together, care for one another, follow rules, do jobs around the home, respect one another, and have fun. Being kind also helps everyone in the family get along. What do you do to help make your family a kinder, happier community?

I show kindness to my family when I...

- give compliments from my heart
- look after my younger sister or brother
- spend time having fun with my parents
- show interest in what my parents do
- tell my family that I love them
- learn about my family history from my grandparents
- clean my room and help around the house

I love playing chess with my dad. I play other games with my mom and my brothers and sisters.

I read books to my brother and help him learn to read books on his own.

My brother walks using a walker. I love taking him outside and walking with him.

My family members love to hug one another! It makes us feel loved.

What makes a kind friend?

Your parents, brothers, and sisters can be your friends, as well as the kids at your school.

Friends are people we love to be with. They can be members of our family, the kids at school, and people with whom we play music or sports. Friends are not always the same as we are. They can be older or younger and belong to different **cultures**. The children below are holding signs showing what they think makes a kind friend. Write down the names of your friends and the reasons you like each one. What is the kindest thing a friend has ever done for you?

A kind friend is someone who...

Kindness compliments for friends

Getting compliments makes people happy, but giving them also makes us feel happy. Saying something nice, such as "I like your new haircut," can make someone feel good, but saying something positive about a person's character can make him or her feel wonderful! A compliment that comes from the heart means a lot. Read the examples below. Then say or write them to your friends, teachers, parents, and other family members. How did they react? How did sharing those compliments make you feel?

- Thank you for being such a wonderful friend.
- I appreciate the things you do for me and others.
- I love the way you treat everyone with respect.
- You are one of the most creative people I know.
- You always have great ideas.
- You have so many talents. I especially love your art.
- You're a great athlete who always shows team spirit.
- I admire how fair you are to others.
- Thank you for helping me with my schoolwork. You are really smart, and you work so hard!
- Your stories inspire me.
- You are a great singer.
- Your music makes me jump and dance.

Kindness at school

Being a kindness butterfly will make a big difference in your school community. You and your butterfly classmates can create a better life at school. Have a meeting each morning and talk about how you can practice the important ideas in the box below. At the end of the day, write down all the good things that happened that day. Together, repeat your goal, "Let's make everyone's life better with kindness."

Kindness: We can show kindness by smiling, being friendly, giving compliments, and helping others.

Gratitude: When we live our lives with gratitude, we feel very thankful. Write down three things each day that you are grateful for at school and say "Thank you" often.

Respect: Respect is showing that we admire others, even if we do not share their beliefs or cultures.

Connection: When we work as a team, we have similar goals and values. We feel connected. We can do anything!

Love: Love heals. We need to treat everyone the same as we treat the people we love.

Being positive: Negative thoughts, words, and actions hurt us and others! Positive thoughts, words, and actions help us as well as others.

Generosity: When we share what we have, we help others. Our kind words are gifts, too.

Empathy: Empathy is showing concern for the feelings of others and trying to understand what they are feeling. Listening to others and helping them shows empathy.

Write down the names of five people who work at your school. Find out three things they do to make your school a better place. Then, with a group of friends, make thank-you cards to thank them for those and all the other things they do to help students. Your school community helpers will be very pleased with your gratitude and kindness.

Do you have a music teacher at your school? What kind comments would you like to share with him or her?

How does playing sports make you feel? How would you thank your coach for teaching you how to play soccer? Why is the exercise you get while playing soccer important to your health?

How can you show empathy to someone with special needs? How is this girl helping her friend?

Kindness in my community

A community is a place where many people live and work together. There are many problems in the world today. We need to change the way we think, act, and live. When we work together, we can do anything! The best place to start is in our community. Acts of kindness can spread quickly! In what ways could you be helpful in your community? Are there clothes, books, or toys you could donate?

This girl is donating some of her hair to a place that makes wigs for cancer patients who have lost their hair.

Some of the girl's hair was used to make a wig for a woman who lost her hair.

Find out how you can volunteer in your community. Helping others will make you feel good about yourself.

These girls are exercising with an older neighbor. They are having fun helping her keep fit. They also enjoy going for walks with her and her dog.

Gratitude butterflies

Gratitude is feeling thankful from the bottom of your heart. When you feel gratitude for the things in your life, you feel happy to be alive. You feel loved. Having an attitude of gratitude helps change negative feelings to positive ones. Just as with kindness, you can be a gratitude butterfly that flaps appreciation to others. When you pay attention to what is good in your life instead of what is bad, you have more positive emotions. When you are positive, you feel happier, and so do the people around you.

Gratitude creates a good feeling in your heart.

Practicing gratitude makes people think of us in a positive way. Expressing gratitude to our friends can improve our friendships. Sharing gratitude makes everyone feel happier.

Gratitude makes us aware of all the things our bodies and minds do. When you know how your body works, you can't help but praise every part for doing its job so well!

Start a gratitude journal and write down five things each day for which you are thankful.

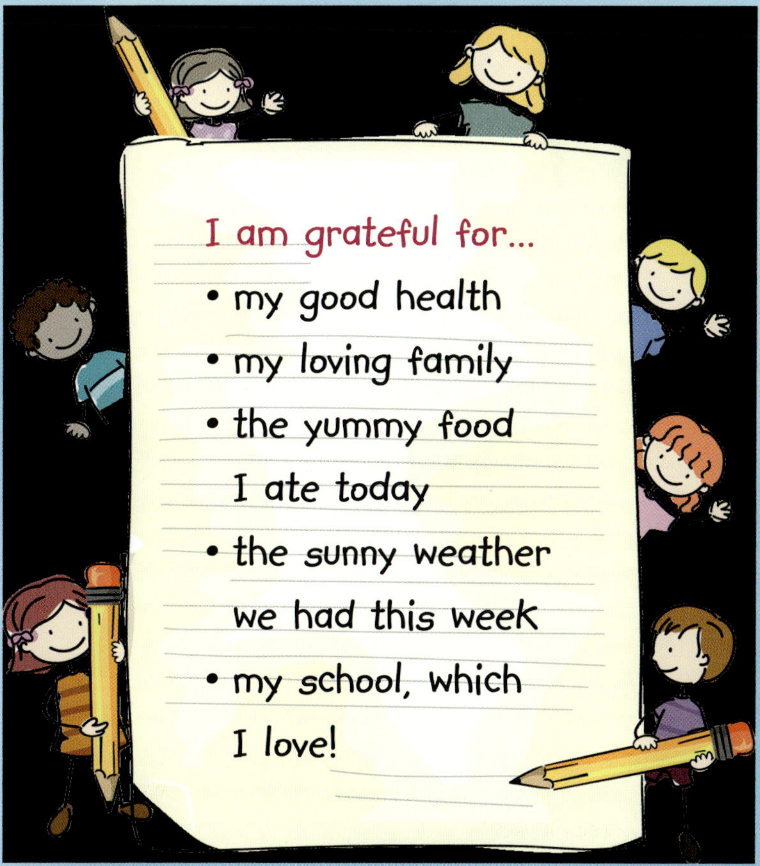

Diversity means variety. The world is made up of a variety of people. Each person is **unique**, or one of a kind, and different. We have different faces, different talents, and different dreams. We may have different cultures and beliefs, wear different clothes, or speak different languages. When we forget that we are connected, we often pull away from one another. We may even hurt one another. We are more alike than we are different, but sometimes we see only our differences. If we were all the same, can you imagine how boring the world would be?

We have different cultures and religions. We can learn from one another. We are all important!

Inclusion is welcoming diversity and including different kinds of people to create a happy life for everyone. Sometimes we forget that we are more alike than we are different. We need the same things and are connected to one another because we all live on Earth. How can we be inclusion butterflies? We can get to know one another! Getting to know people from different cultures is a great way to learn about the world. We need to look beyond how we are different and make it our goal to work together.

We are the same and different.
How are differences interesting
and fun?

Why is kindness cool?
How can we help one another?
How can we show that we care?

We are the Earth!

Earth is the only planet in our **solar system** that has life. Only Earth has plants, animals, people, and other living things. Only Earth has air, water, and food. Earth is just the right distance from the Sun, too. The Sun gives all living things on Earth enough light and warmth to stay alive. Every person, animal, and plant shares Earth. We are a part of everything, and everything is a part of us.

Climate change

Human activities use up Earth's **natural resources**, such as water. We also create pollution and add to the problems of **climate change**. Scientists believe human activity is slowly increasing Earth's temperature. Even the smallest changes in temperature can create big changes in our environment, such as extreme weather that leads to **drought** or flooding. Many countries are trying to fix the problems caused by climate change.

You and your friends can work together to help Earth. Start with the three Rs: reduce, reuse, and recycle!

How can we be eco-friendly?

When we are eco-friendly, we do not hurt Earth or ourselves. Even making a few changes in our lives can make a big difference! As more people make changes, the world will become a cleaner, safer, more peaceful place for all living things.

- To be eco-friendly in winter, open your curtains to let the Sun help heat your home. Turn down the heat and wear a sweater.
- In summer, close the curtains to stop heat from coming in.
- Turn off the water while you brush your teeth.
- Take quick showers.
- Turn off the lights when you leave a room.
- Buy fruit that is grown close to home. Trucks that bring food from far away create pollution by burning a lot of gas.
- Walk or use a bike to keep the air clean.

Plant trees in your yard or community. Planting trees helps clean the air.

Kindness after disasters

These children escaped from their country by crossing the sea by boat.

Bad weather is a huge problem in many places around the world. People have lost their homes due to floods, tornadoes, hurricanes, and forest fires. Many people have also had to escape wars and unsafe living conditions in their countries. Having to move to a new country is difficult, especially if you do not speak the same language.

This boy is living in a refugee camp.

Who needs our help?

People who have lost their homes often have no place to live, clothes to wear, or food to eat. The following are examples of people who may need the help of others:

- **Refugees** are people who have left their country to escape wars or natural disasters.
- **Immigrants** are people who have left their country permanently and are living in a new country.
- **Migrants** are people who move from place to place to find better jobs and homes.
- **Evacuees** are people who have been forced to move to safer places due to hurricanes, floods, fires, or other natural disasters.

These migrant children have been separated from their parents and are helping one another with smiles and hugs.

Living with fear

After something terrible happens, children may feel frightened, sad, or angry. Children who have experienced **trauma**, or a very stressful experience, need to trust in order to feel safe again.

Needing our kindness

Helping others makes us feel good, and it brings kindness back into our own lives. Are there people you know who could use some kind words or acts? The smallest act of kindness can change a person's life! How powerful is that? Decide to perform at least one kind act each day. The more acts of power you perform, the more powerful you will become!

Do you have children at your school or in your community who do not speak English? Try teaching them some words, or help them learn to read. You could also invite them to go for a walk in the park or play sports or music with you and your friends.

You can donate clothes, books, and toys to local organizations that help people. You can become a volunteer, as well.

Your kindness challenge

By taking time to be kind to others, you will not only give them a better day, but their gratitude will make your day better, too. Happiness is spread through each and every one of us. We connect with others through kindness. Challenge yourself to do at least five acts of kindness each day, such as the ones shown on these pages.

Give flowers to your grandmother.

Smile at people you meet, and laugh with your friends. Smiling and laughing make you happy, and they make others happy, too.

Hug a pet and feel the love in your heart. Treat others with that kind of love.

Remember that being a kindness butterfly can change your life and the lives of others. Flap your kindness wings and help change the world!

Glossary

Note: Some boldfaced words are defined where they appear in the book.

adopted Legally raised as one's own

aware Having knowledge or being well-informed

climate change The change in the normal weather conditions due to greenhouse gases, such as carbon dioxide

community A group of people who live or work together

contagious Spread from person to person

culture The customs and traditions of a group of people

diversity Variety

drought A long period of time without rain or with very little rain

extended A family that includes more than parents and children

illustrate To show or explain

impact To have an effect on someone or something

inclusion The act of including different kinds of people

ingredients Foods or substances used in a certain dish

natural resources Materials or substances found in nature

solar system The eight planets and their moons that move around the Sun

trauma A very disturbing experience

unique One of a kind; unlike anyone else

Index